3-10

DATE DUE

Roy Raccoon

Dave and Pat Sargent are longtime residents of Prairie Grove, Arkansas. Dave, a fourth-generation dairy farmer, began writing in early December 1990, and Pat, a former teacher, began writing shortly after. They enjoy the outdoors and have a real love for animals.

Roy Raccoon

By

Dave and Pat Sargent

Illustrated by
Jean Lirley Huff

Ozark Publishing, Inc.
P.O. Box 228
Prairie Grove, AR 72753

iii

Library of Congress Cataloging-in-Publication Data

Sargent, Dave, 1941-
    Roy Raccoon / Dave and Pat Sargent ; illustrated by Jean Huff.
        p. cm. — (Animal pride series ; 1)
        Summary: A young raccoon learns skills for surviving in the wild. Includes facts about   the physical characteristics, behavior, habitat, and predators of the raccoon.
        ISBN 1-56763-005-7. — ISBN 1-56763-077-4 (alk. paper)
        1. Raccoons—Juvenile fiction. [1. Raccoons—Fiction.] I. Sargent, Pat, 1936- .
        II. Huff, Jean, ill. III. Title. IV. Series: Sargent, Dave, 1941- Animal pride   series ; 1.
        PZ10.3.S243Ro   1996
        [Fic]—dc20
        96-1499
        CIP
        AC

Printed in the United States of America

Inspired by

a pet coon I had when I was a child.

Dedicated to

my good buddy, Andrew Happy.

Foreword

Roy Raccoon is an adventurous little raccoon. He is always getting into something. When Mama Raccoon takes her cubs to a nearby stream for a lesson on how to catch fish, Roy's curiosity gets the best of him, and he gets his paw caught in a trap. Mama Raccoon tells him that she will have to chew off his paw if he is to ever get free.

Contents

Roy Raccoon

If you would like to have the authors of the Animal Pride Series visit your school, free of charge, call 1-800-321-5671 or 1-800-960-3876.

One

Roy Raccoon

Now that Roy Raccoon was three months old, he and his brother and two sisters went hunting with their mama every night. They lived in a big white oak tree that was hollow in the center. The entrance to their nest was about twenty feet above the ground. They always slept during the day and hunted for food at night.

Roy woke up in late afternoon, just about sundown. His sisters, Jane and Amber, and his brother, Jim, were still asleep. Roy nudged Jim with his front paw and said,

"Hey, Jim, wake up. It's almost time to go hunting."

Jim just lay there, sound asleep. He wasn't in any hurry to get up.

Roy nudged his brother again with his front paw, and said, "Come on, Jim. Let's go out and play on the tree limbs. It's no fun playing all by myself."

Roy kept trying to wake Jim, but it was no use. He said, "Jim, you're an old sleepy head!"

Roy sat on the side of his bed and thought, "I know what I'll do. I'll wake Jane and Amber. Maybe they'll want to get up and play with me."

Roy Raccoon went over to where Amber and Jane were sleeping. He poked them and said, "Come on, girls. It's time to get up and go hunting."

At first, there was no response.

3

He shook them again and said, "Come on. It's time to get up. Let's go play on the tree limbs until Mama wakes up."

Amber rolled over and stretched. Then she slowly opened her eyes. "Roy," she asked, "why are you waking me? Why don't you leave me alone? I'm sleepy."

"I want to play, Amber," Roy said. "Come play with me."

Amber said, "You're sure making a lot of noise. You're waking everyone up."

"It's time to go hunting, any way," Roy stated. "So, wake up!"

"Where is Mama?" Amber asked.

"She's sleeping in her part of the tree," Roy re plied.

"Well," Amber said, "if it was time to get up, Mama would be here. If you don't leave me alone and let me sleep, I'm going to tell Mama." She lay down and closed her eyes.

It wasn't long until she was asleep.

Roy Raccoon said, "I'll go outside and play by myself." He crawled through the small hole and onto a limb of the big white oak tree.

Roy had hoped that it would be dark so they could go hunting, but it was still light. The sun had gone down, and there was a beautiful sunset, with the sky in the west turning a reddish gold.

He lay on top of a limb for a long time, watching the sunset fade from reddish gold to a dull gray. It wasn't long until a dark blanket covered the sky. The moon was not yet up when Roy thought, "It's going to be a dark night if the moon doesn't come up."

Roy began running up and down the tree and out on the limbs.

He was chattering and shaking the small limbs and making all kinds of noise.

After several minutes, Roy's mother stuck her head out of a hole in the big oak tree. She asked, "Roy, what are you doing?"

"I'm playing," Roy replied.

"Well, you are certainly making a lot of noise. You are waking everyone up," she said, with a frown on her face.

"It's time to go hunting," Roy stated. "Let's go!"

"Not yet," his mother replied. "We're not going hunting until the moon comes up. That's still two hours away. Go back to bed and get some more sleep."

Yes, Mama," Roy said. He crawled back into the nest and lay down. He lay there for a long time before finally falling asleep.

It seemed to Roy that he had

not been asleep any time before Mama Raccoon stuck her head through the door. She said, "Okay, everyone, it's time to get up. Come on, let's go."

One by one, the young cubs stretched and yawned and woke up. After three or four minutes, they were fully awake and ready to go.

Two

The Trap

Mama Raccoon looked at the cubs and said, "Tonight we are going fishing. I am going to show you how to catch fish. You must remember to be very quiet at all times, because the slightest noise will scare the fish away."

The stream was quite aways from the raccoons' home. The family of raccoons could hear dogs barking as they slowly made their way toward the stream.

When the sounds of the dogs drew nearer and nearer, Mama Raccoon

said, "Those dogs mean trouble.
Let's run as fast as we can! Once we
get to the creek, we can lose the
dogs in the water."

Mama Raccoon and the cubs ran very quickly now. When they reached the stream, the dogs were not far behind. Mama Raccoon said, "Come on, kids, follow me. We'll swim downstream so that the dogs can't trail us." Mama Raccoon and the cubs jumped into the water and started swimming downstream.

When the dogs reached the stream, they ran up and down the bank, trying to pick up the raccoons' trail. After a time, they gave up and headed away from the creek.

Mama Raccoon and the four cubs made their way to the bank on the other side of the creek. There they realized that the dogs had turned back. They shook the water from their coats. Then they quickly groomed their fur with their paws. Now, they were ready to go fishing.

Mama Raccoon said, "Now remember, kids, you must be very quiet."

They moved downstream a short distance to a shallow hole of water. With her experienced eyes, Mama Raccoon saw several fish. She whispered to the cubs, "Watch me." Never taking her eyes off the fish, she moved close to the water's edge.

As one of the fish swam near the bank, Mama Raccoon grabbed it with her front paws. With her sharp teeth, she pulled the fish from the water and carried it to the cubs. They would eat well tonight.

The cubs asked, "Mama, is this the only fish we are going to catch?"

Mama Raccoon replied, "No, we are going to catch more fish if we are still hungry after we have eaten this one. You must remem ber that you should never catch more fish than you can eat."

After eating the first fish, Mama Raccoon said, "Now, watch me. I'm going to catch another one."

The cubs watched as Mama Raccoon caught the second fish. After they had eaten it, she asked, "Are you still hungry?"

The cubs said, "Yes."

Mama Raccoon told the cubs, "Each of you must now try catching a fish all by your self."

Each cub took up a place at the

edge of the stream. When a fish swam by, they would try to catch it. They were not having any luck. They didn't have the speed that their mother had, and they were not as fast with their paws.

The cubs kept trying. Before long, Roy thought to himself, "This fishing is not much fun. I think I'll find something else to do." He looked down the stream and saw a log lying across the stream. He thought, "I'll get on that log, and maybe the fishing will be better."

Roy Raccoon hurried down stream and climbed onto the log. As he started walking across it, he looked down into the water. All the fish were swimming to the other end of the pool. They could see Roy Raccoon crossing the log. They knew what he was doing. Roy realized that he couldn't catch any fish that way, so he decided to play.

While he was running back and forth across the log, he suddenly saw something shiny. The shiny thing

was down in a hole in the log. He
stopped and looked down.

Roy Raccoon didn't know that Andy, a young boy who lived on a nearby farm, wanted a coonskin hat. He had drilled a hole about an inch across and three inches deep in the log where Roy was playing. After drilling the hole, Andy had driven three nails into the log, at an angle, so that the sharp points of the nails were sticking out in the hole. Then he had placed some shiny foil in the bottom of the hole. He knew that a raccoon could not resist trying to get the shiny foil out.

Well, that is exactly what Roy did. He stuck his paw into the hole and reached down past the nails. The points of the nails scrapped against his paw as he reached for the foil.

When Roy tried to pull his paw

from the hole, the nails pierced the skin on his paw. He was hung on the nails. He couldn't get his paw out of the hole.

Three

Billy Beaver Helps Roy

Roy Raccoon yelled, "Mama, Mama, help me! My paw is caught in a hole and I can't get it out!"

Mama Raccoon and all the cubs ran to help Roy. Mama Raccoon tried pulling on Roy's paw, but that didn't help. The harder she pulled, the deeper the nails went into his paw.

Mama Raccoon didn't know what to do. Every time she pulled on Roy's paw, he screamed with pain! The nails were hurting him.

Mama Raccoon tried clawing

and chewing the log, hoping to free Roy's paw, but it was no use. The log was too hard, and her teeth were not made for chewing on wood. Mama Raccoon kept trying. She was not about to give up.

After a time, Roy's mama said, "It's just no use. I can't free your paw, Roy. I'm afraid it's hopeless. The only thing I know to do is to chew your paw off. That's the only way to get it loose. You will have only three legs, but at least you will be alive and free."

"Oh no, Mama! Please don't! Please don't chew my paw off," Roy pleaded. "I don't want to lose my paw. Please try to get help, Mama."

Mama Raccoon thought for a minute, then said, "I know. There's a beaver pond just downstream only a short distance from here. Beavers have long, sharp teeth made for chewing on wood. I'll run down and see if I can find Billy Beaver."

Mama Raccoon took off, running downstream. She got to the

edge of the beaver pond, and there was Billy Beaver working on the dam by moonlight.

Mama Raccoon hollered, "Billy! Billy Beaver! I need your help!"

Billy Beaver stopped what he was doing and swam to the backside of the pond to meet Mama Raccoon. He climbed out of the water and shook himself, being careful not to get Mama Raccoon wet.

Billy said, "Hello, Mrs. Raccoon. You seem very upset. Is something wrong?"

"Roy's paw is caught in a hole in a log," Mama Raccoon said exciedly. "The log is lying across the stream just a short distance from here. I can't get his paw out, Billy. I thought you might be able to get him loose with your long, sharp teeth."

"Roy is my friend. I'll see what I can do," Billy said. They hurried upstream.

When Billy saw what the problem was, he went to work on the log. He chewed and chewed. It was hard and dry, which made it very difficult for him to chew. However, he kept working away.

Billy Beaver's teeth were very sharp. With each bite, more chips fell from the log. Finally, Roy Raccoon's paw was free.

Roy's paw was already sore where the sharp nails had pierced his skin.

Mama Raccoon looked Roy's paw over real good. She said, "Your paw will be all right, Roy. Now, don't stick it in anything else."

Everyone thanked Billy Beaver for saving Roy's paw, especially Roy. He said, "I'll be forever grateful to you, Billy."

Billy Beaver went back to his pond, and Mama Raccoon took her cubs and headed for their home in the big hollow white oak tree.

Four

Raccoon Facts

The raccoon is a bushy, ringed tail animal with a band of black around its eyes. The black around the eyes looks like a mask. An adult raccoon will have from five to seven rings around its tail.

Raccoons live both on the ground and in trees. They are found in North America and South America. There are two main species, the northern raccoon and the crab-eating raccoon.

The northern raccoon lives in Canada, the United States, and Central America. The crab-eating raccoon lives in Costa Rica, Panama, and South America. Several kinds of raccoons live on tropical islands.

Both northern and crab-eating raccoon eat crabs. Their other food includes crayfish, frogs, fish, and other freshwater animals. Raccoons also eat acorns, birds' eggs, corn, fruit, nuts, seeds, and small land animals, such as grasshoppers and mice.

Some people believe that raccoons dunk food in water to wash it, but scientists believe that they are simply imitating the way they would pull fish or other ani mals from rivers and streams. They do not believe that raccoons actually wash their food.

Northern raccoons mate once a year between January and June. About nine weeks after mating, the female has from one to eight babies. A baby raccoon is called a cub.

Newborn raccoons have no mask around their eyes or rings around their tails. Their eyes do not open until about twenty days after birth. The mother protects her young and does not even let the father near them. The babies stay in the den from eight to ten weeks.

Raccoons are more intelligent than cats and can be easily trained, but after they reach the age of about 1 year, they may be easily angered and, as a result, often bite and scratch.